D0512071

St Felix for the Cup!

Shoo Rayner

h

Hodder
Children's
Books

a division of Hodder Headline plc

First published in Great Britain in 1996
by Hodder Children's Books, a division of Hodder Headline plc
338 Euston Road
London NW1 3BH

Copyright © 1996 Shoo Rayner

The right of Shoo Rayner to be identified as the Author of this Work has been asserted by him in
accordance with the Copyright, Designs and Patents Act 1988.

ISBN 0340 619589

10 9 8 7 6 5 4 3 2

A catalogue record for this title is available from the British Library

Printed and bound in Great Britain by
Cox and Wyman Ltd, Reading, Berks.

Chapter 1

It was the first day of the
holidays. The sun streamed into
Ginger's room and woke him.
He lay in bed for a while, just
thinking. There was no morning
rush to school today.

While he was eating his
breakfast, his mum told him
about her plans for the holidays.

Ginger's mum thought that
Tiddles was the best behaved
kitten she knew because he
always said nice things about
her cooking!

Ginger walked round to see Tiddles. It was such a lovely day, he whistled loudly and thought to himself.

It's true, Tiddles had once been the school bully. He had been pretty mean to Ginger, but with his grandad's help, Ginger had learned to stand up for himself. In fact he'd become so brave that his friends started calling him The Ginger Ninja.

Last term, the two kittens had been made to work together in the school play and somehow they'd become the best of friends.

When Tiddles answered the door, Ginger didn't give him time to say hello.

Guess what? My mum says you can come on holiday with us to my gran's. She lives by the sea, and it's really great there, there's so much to do on the beach and everything. Please say you can come. I mean – you do think your parents will let you?

Yeah, I hope so. Let's go and ask.

Tiddles's mum wasn't sure.

They waited all day for Mr
Tailer to come home, and
listened at the door as Tiddles's
mum told him about the holiday.

Chapter 2

They had to wait two weeks, but
finally the day came. Ginger
helped Tiddles squeeze his bag
into the boot.

Mrs Tailer gave Tiddles
a big kiss. She stood
on the pavement and
waved until they
were completely
out of sight.

As soon as they drove off Mr and Mrs Pickles started talking and didn't stop until they got to Granny's house.

Well she is getting on a bit and I don't know how long she can go on living on her own in that house etcetera, blah, blah, blah

Yes, dear

They drove out of town...

HOLIDAY ROUTE

along the motorway...

Sat in a traffic jam for hours...

and tootled down country lanes for a few hours...

until they got to Granny's house.

Granny was nice.

Ginger loved
his granny.
She was a really
good cook so
Tiddles liked her too!

This'll be your
room, boys.

The two kittens shared the room
in the attic. Through
its tiny window
Tiddles got his
first ever view
of the sea.

Wow!

Let's go!

While the grown-ups carried on
talking, Ginger and Tiddles went
exploring.

There were gigantic trees that
needed to be climbed and endless
fields to be walked through.

There were
cliffs to be
scaled.

Caves to
be entered.

But best of all there was the beach.
(Of course they didn't go
swimming . . . cats don't
like getting wet!)

They ran about . . .

buried themselves . . .

made sand castles . . .

flew kites . . .

and practised pawball
shots for hours.

They had the most wonderful
holiday, but all good things must
come to an end. They spent the
rest of the holidays practising
pawball in the park at home.
It was fun but not as good as the
beach.

Chapter 3

At the start of the new term there was great excitement at St Felix's as the list for the Pawball Squad was pinned up on the notice board. Ginger and Tiddles were on it.

They practised all sorts of routine plays.

Ginger's grandpa was the unofficial team coach. He gave them a morale-boosting chat.

Chapter 4

Before the match Tiddles went quite moody . . .

and niggley . . .

and short-tempered . . .

and quiet . . .

and sullen.

The rest of the team commented on his change of behaviour but Ginger stood up for him.

The Feral Street Team arrived.
They were HUGE!

Tiddles was marked by a big
kitten called Flossie.

She hardly gave him room to
stand up and made him look
completely useless.

Feral Street didn't exactly play
by the rules. They tripped and
kicked and pinched and held.

During one play the kittens piled
on top of each other so no one
saw what happened to Tiddles
but they all suspected Flossie had
something to do with it.

Poor Tiddles had to be carried off
on a stretcher. Flossie cheered
him off the pitch.

Chapter 5

As Tiddles didn't come to school
for the next couple of days,
Ginger went round to see him.
Mrs Tailer answered the door.

When he did come back to
school he just sulked.

Ginger worried about his friend.

Ginger brought some fishybix to school and went looking for Tiddles. He found him sulking in a tree.

However bad he felt, Tiddles could always eat a fishybik.

Tiddles looked at his feet for a
while then, with a deep sigh, he
started to pour out his troubles.

I couldn't take any more so I hit her.

No one believed that she was bullying me because she was a girl.

So I got sent here instead.

Well, all I knew was how to bully. If nothing else Flossie taught me how to do that and you know the rest.

Then, when we played Feral Street, it all came back to me.

Oh Tiddles, that's terrible. Never mind, we'll work it out.

So that was it. Since they had become such good friends, Ginger couldn't understand why Tiddles had been so horrible to him at first. Now it all made sense – Tiddles had never known how to be friends before.

Chapter 6

Ginger had a plan, but he wasn't sure whether Grandpa would approve of it.

Grandpa?
You remember before Tiddles and I were friends? And remember you gave me an invisible amulet? You said it would protect me and help me to become the Ginger Ninja ... well ... it was a sort of trick, wasn't it?

I suppose it was ... sort of. But you believed in it and it helped you to believe in yourself, that's what was important.

Ginger told Grandpa all about
Tiddles's troubles.

Ginger and Tiddles went for a long walk in the park. When they got to the pond Ginger revealed the secrets of the Ginger Ninja as they skimmed stones across the water.

Ginger made a fuss of taking the invisible amulet from around his neck.

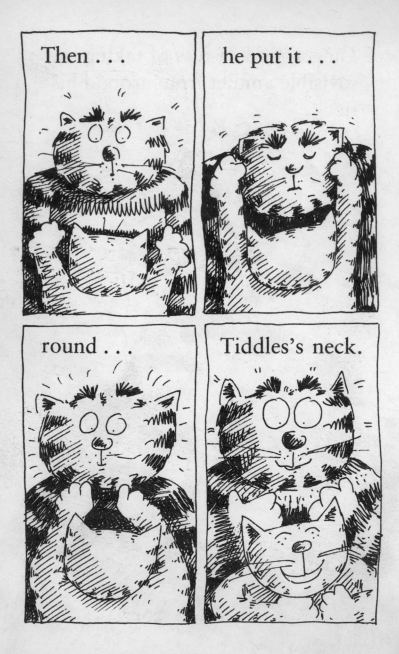

Tiddles was lost for words.

It was like turning on a switch.
Suddenly he was a new kitten,
bursting with enthusiasm and
energy. On the pawball pitch he
was everywhere.

St Felix's team went racing up
the league, easily winning all
their matches.

St Felix's did so well that they soon found themselves in the final. And which team did they find themselves drawn against?

FERAL STREET JUNIOR!

Chapter 7

Even with Ginger's amulet to protect him, Tiddles was nervous.

At the last practice before the
big day, Ginger called the team
together and Tiddles told them
why he had been so useless in the
last match against Feral Street.

The rest of the team were determined to help and thought up ways to deal with the dreaded Flossie.

"No," said Ginger. "We'll have to be really clever and get her sent off. How about if we. . ."

They spent the rest of the practice session rolling around on the grass, clutching their arms and legs in agony. There was some very bad acting!

The big day dawned. The kittens were nervous. They were quiet and thoughtful in the coach that took them to the playing field.

They were quiet and thoughtful in the changing rooms, until the time came to face the "Enemy".

The St Felix supporters cheered.

The Feral Street Supporters booed.

Flossie looked as though she was going to eat Tiddles for tea. Tiddles kept reassuring himself.

The referee waited until
everyone was in their place,
then he blew his whistle, and
threw the pawball up into the air.

Chapter 8

In fairness, it has to be said that Feral Street were quite a good team. They were big, but St Felix's easily matched them in skill.

Being taller, Feral Street could intercept quite easily.

Being bigger and stronger they could throw further.

But, being smaller and nimbler, St Felix's could outmanoeuvre the bigger kittens.

Flossie was the real problem. She was such a brute, and marked Tiddles as if he were her shadow.

So, whenever she came near a St Felix kitten, they pretended she had fouled them!

By half time the whole team
appeared to be wounded.

They were
limping . . .   stooping . . .

groaning . . .   and pretending
                                    to cry.

But
the ref
wasn't
fooled.

The half-time bowls came on and
St Felix's went into a huddle.

Tail holding is not allowed. See page 64.

All through the second half they forced the play into Flossie's quarter. They performed skilful passing plays right in front of Flossie's nose.

They passed behind her . . .

over her . . .

and under her,

and all the time

they wafted

their tails

in front of her.

The game was nearly over and Flossie hadn't taken the bait. She had been kept so busy that she had almost forgotten about Tiddles, until he caught the pawball and made as if to throw it.

Feral St.
20
St Felix
20

He held back the throw as long as he could, while he wiggled and waggled the tip of his tail, like a worm on a fishing hook.

Flossie was determined to stop
him. Mesmerised by Tiddles's
wriggling tail, she quite forgot
herself and reached out to grab it.

The referee blew
his whistle so hard
the pea nearly
came out!

The crowd stood in shocked
silence. Flossie stood in the
middle of the pitch, looking
stupid, holding Tiddles's tail.

Flossie was sent
off, muttering
threats and curses.

Just you wait,
Tiddles!

Tiddles was given a free throw.
He took his time lining up the
shot while Ginger picked up
the goalcatcher. On the beach,
in the summer, they had
practised this shot so
often but now it
was for real.

The pawball
soared way up
high into the
air and seemed
to hang there for
as long as you could hold
your breath. Then it came
hurtling down towards Ginger.

The pawball landed in the catcher with a satisfying thud and Ginger cleanly slammed it into the bin.

The crowd erupted into cheers as the referee blew the whistle for full time. It was all over. St Felix's had won the cup!

Chapter 9

Flossie was livid. To have been duped by Tiddles, of all people.

As the victorious team left the changing rooms, ready for their celebration tea, she was waiting for him.

We won the Cup! We won the Cup!
Eee-I-me-daddy-oh! We won the Cup!

I want a word with you, Tiddles.

He smiled at her. He was with friends that he could trust.

Tiddles
gave
Ginger
a wink.

He took a deep breath,
puffed himself up,
stuck his fur out
and let out a
mighty
roar.

RRAA

For a second Flossie
seemed to have
turned to
stone.

IR

Then she turned and ran as
fast as she could with the
team chasing her until they
couldn't be bothered any more.

RAAAAAAAAAAAAR!

The two teams set about their tea. Without Flossie there, the Feral Street team were quite friendly.
(They really were big though!)

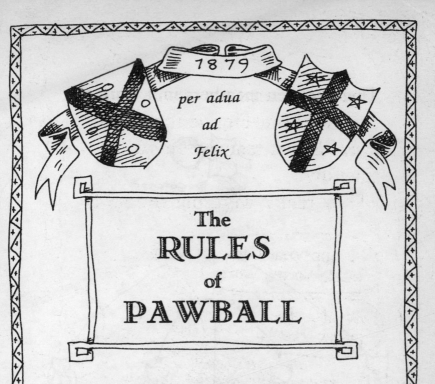

per adua
ad
Felix

1879

The
RULES
of
PAWBALL

Pawball started in back streets, where cats had to make their own fun. They used what materials they could find.

The pawball is a strange shape because it's hard to find anything round or bouncy in a back alley!

The rules have been written down and improved over many years and now it has become the national sport.

There are ten members in a team.

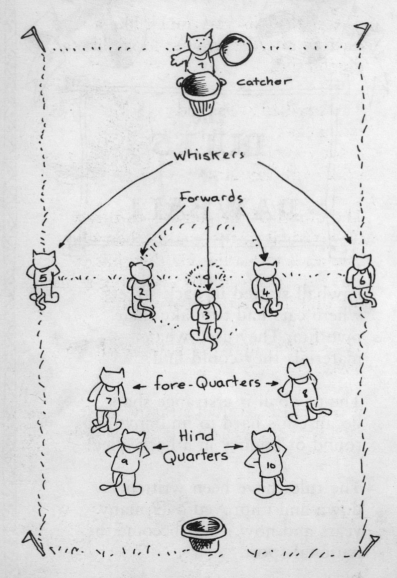

Goal

catcher

The goal looks very much like a dustbin and the catcher looks like a dustbin lid.

The pawball is shaped like a cat's paw. It is made from a leather bag filled with sawdust.

The object of the game is to throw the pawball to the goalcatcher who catches it in his lid. He then has to make the goal safe by clamping it into the bin. This scores two points.

The catcher may not catch with his paws.

If the ball is thrown straight, or it falls into the bin then it scores only one point.

1 pt. Goal.

Throw

catch

slam

2 pt. Goal.

The player with the pawball may not run more than five paces. If it is dropped then possession goes to the other side.

If the goal is touched by the opposite team then there is a free spot goal to be taken from the centre. The thrower may be blocked from two metres away.

A player may be sent off the pitch to cool off for five minutes if the referee thinks that the game is getting too physical.

Blocking is allowed but there should be no physical contact. Players caught tail-holding or pulling will be sent off and a free shot at goal given to the offended player.

© International Pawball Federation